Thank you Sophia, Grant, Taylor, Nick and Zack for listening and sharing your thoughts as I read Hero and Halle's story to you in the early stages. A child's opinion is essential for me when I write children's books. Chase, you are soon to be a big brother. Your innocence with love dances in my heart like Hero and Halle dance with joy.

–S.A.

I would like to dedicate the paintings in this book to Winddancer Glory Halleluja, (Halle) who was my heart dog. She taught me about unconditional love and made every day of her too short life a joy.

–N.H.

Text © 2016 by Susan Amundson
Illustrations © 2016 by Nan Holt
Book Design by Annette Bach, Graphic Design, Inc., Hastings, MN
Edited by Marie Moen, B.S. English and History
All rights reserved, including the right of reproduction in whole or in part in any form.
Bjelkier Press, 1620 Louis Lane, Hastings, MN

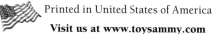 Printed in United States of America
Visit us at www.toysammy.com

Library of Congress Control Number: 2016910003

ISBN: 978-0-9828217-8-7

The text of this book is set in Berkeley Oldstyle Medium.
The illustrations are rendered in acrylic paint on canvas paper.

HERO and HALLE
New Friends

Susan Amundson
Illustrated by **Nan Holt**

Hero is a beautiful Samoyed who can do just about anything.

He can jump over fences

He can pull sleds and smile a Sammy smile.

He gets head pats and even
gets his ears scratched.
LIFE SHOULD NEVER CHANGE,
Hero tells himself.

Then, one day a new dog moves into the neighborhood and brings along a friend. He watches the little dog jump up and sit on the lap of a boy who sits in a chair with wheels.

"Hi. My name is Tony. You are very pretty," he tells Hero as he admires the Samoyed's beautiful fluffy, white hair. "Meet Halle. She's a Silky Terrier, and she's my friend."

Halle stares at Hero and wonders what kind of a neighbor and friend he will be. He's big and scary. He has a dark black nose and black lips that make him look like he's laughing at her. Nope, she tells herself, I'm not going to like him and that's that.

Hero stares at Halle and wonders if he should be her friend. She's little and has hair that looks like silk, but she could never pull sleds.

She's just too little!

"I hope we can all be friends.

I love big, fluffy dogs.
And look, he's smiling at me," says Tony.

Halle feels sad. She's not big and fluffy. Her hair droops because that's what Silky Terrier's hair does. Now this big, fluffy dog is stealing her friend. I don't like him, and that's that.

He's just too big!

After meeting his new neighbors, Hero prances home. Why did they move to my neighborhood? How can I share my head pats and ear scratches with that little, silky mop?

My life was perfect before they came.

Hero thinks Halle is so different.

Halle thinks Hero is so different.

Tony wants them ALL to be friends!

Hero relaxes. He's tired from meeting the new neighbors. Tony might be OK because he likes big, fluffy dogs. But Halle…we're just too different to be friends.

Suddenly, there's a little bark and a little, wet nose touching Hero's big, wet nose. He must be dreaming. Then one eye opens. NO! He's not dreaming. It's Halle, and she's barking and won't stop.

She needs help—or somebody needs Hero's help!

What should Hero do?

He lies down on his tummy and nudges Halle to ride on his back. Halle hangs on as Hero jumps over the fence to take a short cut and runs fast to help somebody.

Hero sees Tony needs help!

"Oh Halle, thank you for bringing that big, fluffy dog to help me," says Tony. "My chair got stuck in the soft grass and I can't move it, but I have an idea how we can fix my problem."

Quickly, Tony puts Halle's leash around Hero and the Samoyed takes control. He holds the leash as Hero pulls like a sled dog working for his master. Halle pushes, and the chair with wheels slowly rolls out of the soft grass.

Halle is thrilled. She barks her little bark of joy and dances in circles. Hero barks his big bark of joy and runs in circles with Halle.
By helping Tony they know they have done something good and quickly become friends.

Hero and Halle have learned something special.
No matter how different they are on the outside,
they have discovered that it's not important.
Instead, by working together they understand their
insides are alike.

Both of them have good hearts,
and that's what matters the most.

Susan Amundson

Susan Amundson is an author of five other children's books that deliver positive messages with a Samoyed featured.

She resides in Minnesota with her husband and share their home with retired show dog, Jesse, a Samoyed. They have three grown children and four grandchildren.

Nan Holt

Nan Holt is a commercial artist and painter living in central Virginia with her husband and Silky Terrier, Sara. They have two sons, three grandchildren, and by early August, three great grandchildren.

ॐ

Samoyed

The Samoyed is highly intelligent, gentle with a connection to children, and known for that "Sammy Smile". This medium-sized sled dog is double coated, stands 19 – 23.5 inches and weighs between 45 – 65 pounds.

Silky Terrier

The Silky Terrier has been described as a big dog in a little dog's suit. While classified as a toy, the Silky is a spunky companion and when allowed, a dedicated varmint hunter. Loyal and friendly with a beautiful silver-blue and tan coat, the Silky is actually born black and tan, changing gradually as it matures. Silky Terriers are very bright and inquisitive. They need activities to occupy them or they may get into trouble.